The Manuscript

A Novella

Lisa Rae Yamagishi

For the tortured poets.

With endless thanks to our poetry department chairman,
Dr. Taylor Alison Swift
for your eternally inspiring lyricism and music!

The 13 Chapter Playlist

1. The Albatross
2. Welcome To New York
3. The Great War
4. Back To December
5. The Prophecy
6. Never Grow Up
7. Peace
8. Peter
9. Fortnight
10. Coney Island
11. The Bolter
12. The Manuscript
13. How Did It End?

"Love is so short, forgetting is so long."

- Pablo Neruda

Chapter 1

The Albatross

Alison sat alone on the front steps of the Albatross Hotel watching the sweaty tourists saunter by, all unaware of her blue eyes glazed with tears. It was the middle of August 1922, and Coney Island was busy and loud during the hot summer season. The small but fancy hotel sat on the edge of the boardwalk along the depths of the Atlantic Ocean, and there was a relentless heat spell that had lasted longer than anyone could remember. No reprieve in the evening to cool off, it had been 13 dangerous hot and stifling days, with no break…

The Albatross Hotel had earned its nickname *"The Lover House"* for its romantic warmth and class it brought to the rich city dwellers who came to Coney Island - perfect for the people who needed to escape the restless boredom that summer heat can sometimes bring.

Alison breathed in the humid air filled with the stench of sweat mixed with ocean air, seaweed, and fried food. The crowds walking along the boardwalk were in disbelief at the heat. She envied them for being able to escape to the beaches and pools, but she felt trapped in the swelter, becoming a victim of the sun every day.

Before the summer began, Alison was supposed to be sent away. She was still a teenager, and her parents had planned with her doctor for her to be sent to the sanitarium. They didn't understand how she could always be so emotional and erratic. Alison experienced very eccentric highs and low lows. She was a problem in their eyes, and they didn't know how to deal with her. They were worried about appearances and embarrassed their daughter was considered unstable. Her parents' friends had started to gossip about the unstable child, and it was becoming an issue for their social circle. They had planned the sanitarium hospital treatments a few months earlier after speaking with the doctor. It was common practice back then and was viewed as a cure for many ailments in young women. Alison wasn't aware of the true extent of what was going to happen to her, but she knew she didn't want to find out. So, on the morning of the scheduled intake to the hospital, Alison climbed out her bedroom window and ran as fast and far away as she could.

Somehow, a week later, she found herself on Coney Island, standing in front of the Albatross Hotel staring at a "Musician Wanted" sign on the front door. Her whole body was filled with nerves and excitement.

Alison loved music and was a talented piano player and singer growing up. Music and writing were the only things that made her feel better when the rest of the world felt confusing and cold.

She had felt as though she struck gold when she applied and got the gig. The audition was just between her and the hotel owner, and it lasted only one minute before he told her she was hired. She would play piano and sing during dinner time, sometimes going late into the night. Room and board at the hotel were included, which was convenient considering Alison was now homeless.

August, the owner of the hotel, was the one who hired Alison. He was a beam of light in his late thirties, and Alison had unwittingly and quickly fallen in love with him when she realized he truly believed in her. He had become her obsession. August was handsome, kind, and tall, and beamed a sense of security and warmth to Alison. She had started to develop thoughts and fantasies that completely revolved around him, lingering and languishing, enveloped with the idea of having him love her back.

By the end of July, August had become like a drug for Alison - a narcotic. When she saw him, her heart raced and it felt like she had been struck with lightning, a cosmic encounter. Alison knew she had put August on a pedestal - she *knew* no man was perfect, but she could not get him out of her head or her heart. He made her so nervous, like a rush to the head, the blood flowed violently throughout her body. She felt the most alive anytime he entered the lobby.

It didn't take much time for August to figure out that Alison wanted to be with him, which made everything complicated considering he had started to have feelings for her while listening to her sing and play piano every night. He became entranced and hypnotized with her music. The way Alison looked at August was unlike anything he had ever seen before, and he liked it. Her innocence intrigued him, and he could tell she was lost and alone in the world. He didn't know where she had come from, she had kept her history vague to him. Alison believed everything he said to her and listened to him so intently. Her vulnerability and naïvety made August feel powerful and needed. She was like a small puppy who followed him blindly.

The twirl of his gold wedding ring reflected sunlight onto the wine glasses hanging in the hotel bar as he caught himself staring at Alison singing.

One night, once Alison had finished performing and the majority of the restaurant had cleared, their hands briefly brushed up against one another. It was the start of what would become a short, intense two-week affair in the middle of the nights. Once the hotel was quiet enough, they would spend all night talking. The clandestine meetings felt dangerous and exciting. Eventually, they would sneak away up to Alison's room. She wished the nights together would never end…

On the 13th night, August decided that it had to end - and fast. He couldn't risk losing his wife, Lucy. August had started to become sick with guilt. He had no idea how this had all happened, but he knew Alison now had the potential to blow up his entire life. He was terrified. He felt like he had become caught up in some kind of spell that Alison had managed to cast upon him. She was a temptress, for only a fortnight, and when that expired, he realized what he had done - as he was overcome with disgust for what he could lose with Lucy. It was clear how strongly Alison had grown to feel for August, and Alison had quickly become a liability. His dreams now consisted of a guilty haunting mixture of Alison and Lucy, their faces blurring together. He would wake up confused, soaked in sweat.

It should be mentioned that Alison felt things more deeply than those around her, the trauma of her past always haunting her present. Alison had very few friends while growing up, and it felt like no one ever wanted to play with her as a little kid. She had always felt like she lived in a shadow of loneliness, only wanting to escape so she could love and be loved. She felt as though she had been left behind in the world, like a prophecy had already strictly sealed her fate – but with August she had felt like she found a soul mate in the middle of those nights together.

Alison's thoughts were stuck in an endless cycle of obsession and intrusive images. Her inner monologue ran furiously in circles, the words pounding into her stomach and heartbeat. Her heart weighed heavily down on her as she still had to face August every night and pretend as though nothing was going on between them. She had started to feel detached from reality, the heat had been getting to her. She felt constantly thirsty and hot. She drifted around Coney Island in a daze during the day, but she continued to sing and play her heart out for the small audiences in the hotel restaurant - and for August. She needed to show him what he might be giving up if he didn't choose her - and she told herself that she could do it with a broken heart.

The guests at the hotel loved Alison's voice. It was sweet and soft, even as the relentless sweat dripped down her neck and long hair. Her cheeks were flushed with blood of nerves and vulnerability. The audience couldn't tell that on the inside, Alison was being tortured and betrayed by her own mind, her nasty inner monologue screaming at her. The poetry she wrote helped ease the burning sting of her aching heart. Her fingers would take it all out onto the keys of her beloved typewriter or her pen. It was the only thing that was truly there for her and loyal to her. She had collected poems, and it had become one of her most prized possessions. Her words meant a lot to her. She knew she was young and had more to experience, but writing made her feel alive and eased her disillusioned thoughts.

Alison didn't have anyone to tell about August, and he knew this. She was isolated on the island, frozen in her distrust of others and her struggle to make friends. She dreamt in her deepest sleep of August holding her in his arms, and in the early mornings, she would awake with a feeling of loss, longing for something that she knew she couldn't keep.

Lucy was beautiful, and her demeanor was the exact opposite of Alison's. She watered flowers in the hotel garden every day and smiled all the time to everyone she saw. Her baby bump had transformed her into one of those women who looked as though they were made to carry a child. She was gorgeous, her laugh was infectious, with her dirty blonde hair falling over her shoulders.

Alison wanted to kill her…

Chapter 2

Welcome To New York

Betty peered out of the window of her tiny dorm room, looking up above at the skyline of the sparkling high-rise buildings of Manhattan. It was December, and red Christmas lights glimmered and shone over New York City. Light bounced dimly against the dirty snow piled onto the edge of the sidewalks. Sirens blared in the distance - clashing with endless taxis honking, each blaring car blending into the melody of the next.

The sky was dark, the moon was new and there were no clouds to reflect the city lights. Betty missed being able to see the stars in the night sky, but she loved being able to look into people's windows. She enjoyed being able to see into the lit-up apartments and offices way across the distance and wondered what everyone was doing beyond their tiny windows. Were they happy? Bored? Lonely? To compensate for her homesickness and overall feeling of awkward anxiety and doom-filled thoughts, Betty relished in her imagination of the mystery of others' experiences. But whenever she peered into the windows, she always thought about one person from her past: James. She hoped that maybe, just maybe, he might be inside one of those windows, staring back at her, with his heart also racing.

At midnight Betty would turn seventeen. She had big hopes that the world would finally treat her a bit differently in the great unknown mystery and future of young adulthood. She wanted to be viewed as mature and grown-up. She wanted to walk into a room and be able to feel completely confident. Most of all, she longed to feel fearless in the world around her.

Betty had been depressed and lonely during the past four months of her freshman year at university. The sparkle and motivation she had felt in high school was no longer there. It was a struggle just to get out of bed in the morning, to shower and get ready for class, to clean, to write, to take care of herself…it all felt like so much and she couldn't keep up with any of it. She isolated herself a lot in the four walls of her dorm room, trying to write, but ended up frustrated and mostly crumpling up papers instead.

It was the very end of her first semester at NYU, and Betty had felt like a small child who had been pretending to be a student. She always felt as though she was faking something. She felt like an actress, pretending to be whatever it was she thought other people might like about her. She had learned to mirror others' energies. Betty was actually a year younger than her peers, but she never shared that information outright with anyone. Nobody could tell, and she didn't want her classmates to know she was younger than them, as she feared she might be treated differently if they knew her secret.

Betty was going back home for the winter holidays tomorrow for three weeks, and she couldn't wait because she had been insanely homesick for the entire semester. Even though she only lived an hour train ride away, it felt like she was living on a different continent while living in the city. She missed her mom and her childhood home so much. She had nostalgia and longed for the comfort and safety of her childhood bedroom.

When Betty looked around campus, it seemed to her as though everyone else was having a great time. Were they all putting on a front? Faking it just like Betty always felt like she was? She was always nervous in class and walking alone around campus. She felt like everyone was always staring at her, secretly laughing and joking about how lonely she looked. While other students always seemed to be so busy, so full of direction and purpose, Betty felt like she had been floundering around throughout the campus, floating and pretending…just surviving. Everyone else appeared to be thriving, happy, and successful everywhere she seemed to go. She felt as though everyone could see right through her, they all could tell that she didn't belong there, like they all knew she was an imposter.

Writing and homework assignments didn't come easy for Betty, and she had a bad habit of procrastinating and then running out of time to finish. The result was rushed assignments with embarrassing mistakes. The professors seemed to enjoy circling the mistakes on her papers with their hostile red pens and handing them back to Betty with a half-disappointed face. It was always confirming what she had been fearing, that she didn't belong and everyone would soon find out that she was not smart enough to be there. Her peers all had such great thoughts and ideas to share in class discussions and group work, but every time Betty felt like she had something even remotely valuable to contribute, the thought of raising her hand and sharing her improvised ideas in front of so many people she didn't know very well made her face burn dark red and her throat tighten. Betty had trouble feeling like she fit into either of the English or Music departments. She often felt stuck in the middle of both worlds.

Betty could tell she had won the roommate lottery living with another Arts major, Inez. She was quirky, but in a cool kind of way. Betty had grown to look up to Inez and couldn't imagine how she would have survived the first semester without her. But when Inez wasn't home, Betty spent a lot of time in her dorm alone with a strange feeling like she was waiting for a train to arrive or for someone to come, but she didn't know what, where, who for, or for how long.

It just so happened that Inez had an older brother named Peter too. He was kind and polite and would come over on Fridays to play games in the girls' dorm. Peter had a girlfriend for the first part of the semester, so Betty had put him in her "no-go category", and had just thought of him as Inez's nice and fun older brother. He had dark hair that cutely fell over his forehead and when he smiled it was always the biggest grin. He was passionate about writing and music too. The first time Betty saw him she immediately liked him. Peter was so friendly to her the first day she moved in with Inez, and he was the very first person who welcomed her to the campus. He opened the door to her new building that day and even helped move Betty's luggage and boxes. She quickly realized that she felt calm around Peter, and she felt like she could be her true self when she was with just Inez and Peter.

Betty felt Inez put a cold glass of wine on her back. It was getting late but Inez was forcing Betty to stay up until midnight for her birthday. Inez had practically forced her cheap rose wine down Betty's throat and had invited Peter over to help them celebrate Betty and the end of the exams. Betty was secretly really happy that Peter was on his way over.

Inez liked to party and Betty was easily influenced by Inez's velour for life. They were too young for bars, so the two would drink in their room and then go on adventures around campus or the park, and eventually "adventure walks" in the city. The night would become a blur of sidewalks, laughter, pizza, and benches.

"They broke up?! Yessss!!" Inez yelled as she was looking down at her phone.

Inez was one of those sisters who dipped her toes too much into her older brother's life. She had been critical of every girlfriend Peter had ever had. No one was good enough for him in her eyes. There was always something wrong with the girl. There was always some type of wrongdoing or drama that had taken place to let Inez know that it wasn't going to work out with any particular girl in her brother's life either.

When Peter arrived, he seemed cheerful for someone going through a breakup.

"Happy birthday Betty!" He cheered.

The three of them drank the rose wine Inez had gotten and had a great time talking and reflecting on stories from the funny nights they remembered from the semester. They stayed up until midnight and celebrated with the cheers of their plastic cups. The two siblings sang happy birthday to Betty - and her face beamed a classic rouge. Being sung to was embarrassing for anyone, but Betty always seemed a little extra sheepish about all the attention.

Betty's birthday had always made her feel a bit sad. She had memories of crying after being overtired from her parties. The end of something she had looked forward to for so long always threw off her emotions. She was always wanting to become older, but dreading the actual day. There was always so much pressure to have the perfect day, and it never seemed to live up to her expectations.

As they all cheered, Betty felt grateful for having met Inez and her brother - it was the first time she felt like she belonged this semester.

"You're only 17 Betty? I thought you were turning 18." Peter interrupted Inez singing the end of Happy Birthday… Inez had let Betty's secret slip.

"I have to get ready for bed!" Inez complained. "I have to work at 7 am tomorrow. Happy birthday Betty! Have a great Christmas break, you better text me a lot. I'll miss you!" She gave Betty a big hug.

Peter was still sitting on Betty's bed. He had found Betty's acoustic guitar that Marjorie had given to her, and was messing around with some chords. Betty liked the music, and she sat back down after giving Inez a farewell hug. She listened to Peter play her guitar. She wasn't sure if Peter was interested in her guitar or just wanted an excuse to talk to her more. In her hopeful mind, it was the latter. By complete accident, Betty's arm grazed against Peter's hand. It was embarrassing for both of them as they realized they had just touched. Betty had never thought of Peter other than Inez's brother until now. Betty could swear that she felt electricity between them. It could have just been static electricity on her flannel bed sheets, but there was a weird feeling between them, and Betty didn't think she was making it up in her head. She wondered if it really was just her imagination or if Peter was feeling something too. She found herself getting lost in Peter's eyes but actively pretending like she didn't think of him any differently than anyone else.

"I guess I should go now, don't want to make little Inez mad! Merry Christmas Betty, thanks for having me tonight!" Peter put the guitar down, grabbed his coat, and was out the door before Betty could say thanks for coming, or to have a good Christmas break. Peter was aloof, and Betty found herself always wanting more. She was sad he had left so abruptly. She could have hung out with him all night long - if given the option.

When Peter was in the room, it always felt brighter and more fun. Betty realized she was starting to really like Peter. She began to worry about what he thought of her and if he liked her back, but she felt like the little sister tag-a-long, rather than a potential girlfriend.

The next morning Betty hauled her ginormous packed suitcase to the train heading home. The train ride flew by quickly and when she got off at her stop her mom hugged her at the train station, and they drove back to the house. The familiarity of the passenger seat of her mom's car and the heat blowing out the vents in front of her made Betty feel warm, happy, and excited for the next few weeks of the break. The stress of final papers, exams, and the final music performance were all behind her now. She had made it through and somehow survived. Everything in this moment felt good and stress-free.

It had been just Betty and her mom since Marjorie had passed. Betty's mom had missed Betty so much. She was constantly torn apart between wanting Betty to have the good and adventurous life she deserved, but also not wanting to let her go and wishing she could hold onto her tighter.

Betty had already told her mom all about Inez and Peter, but she left out the part about her feeling homesick and sad all semester. She didn't want her to know how hard of a time she was secretly having.

Betty opened her bedroom door at home, and it looked just the way she had left it. Her bed was made with extra stuff she hadn't had room to bring. The picture of Marjorie holding her party hat was on Betty's dresser. Her pictures of her high school graduation. Betty's journals tucked away in a box.

Betty felt relief as she lay on her bed.

"Let's go out for dinner tonight, for your birthday!" her mom yelled from the living room.

As Betty and her mom walked towards the door of the restaurant, she looked into the window. A group of young people were all sitting together and laughing with drinks. Betty did a quick glance at each of their faces and got immediately stuck on the back of one of the guy's heads. She felt that familiar feeling she couldn't forget - the chill in her bones of possibly seeing James. She saw him everywhere though, even though it was never him.

The air in the restaurant was cold from the draft of the swinging door and people waiting to be seated. They didn't have to wait too long before they finally got a table. Betty's mom seemed excited to have her back at home, she was more chatty than normal and it was nice.

Before Betty could take her seat, she saw him – and he was walking towards her. She instantly froze and she felt the familiar feeling of her throat tightening. James looked so different. He appeared taller, older, wiser. When he smiled at Betty, she got a shiver up her spine.

"Hello." Her mom said. "Could we get two glasses of water, please?" She didn't realize that this wasn't their waiter.

"It's me, hi-" Betty said, feeling beyond awkward as she heard the three words fall out of her mouth. Of course he knew it was her.

"Hey, Betty." James said back so naturally. "How have you been?"

Betty stared up at James. His eyes were still the same gray-blue she remembered from three years earlier. They hadn't seen each other since their romance had fizzled that June along with Betty's excitement for love. James had graduated and Betty still had two more years of school. He had plans to move to the city and travel, and he had left Betty standing in the dust of their small suburban town. It was ironic that he was now here and Betty was the visitor.

"If we had been closer in age… or maybe in another life. I'm sorry Betty." he had told her that one fateful day, breaking up with her as he left her standing alone on that damn cobblestone sidewalk. It made her want to die with disappointment.

Betty knew she was young but felt like she knew more than people gave her credit for, especially James. She knew he stirred something inside of her that no one else did. He made her feel things that no one else could. Betty would daydream about how maybe they had been connected in another life. Betty thrived in her high school for the next two years without James there to work her up and cause her the intense anxiety she got when she would see him in the hallway. Sure, she had crushes on other boys - but never anything serious. James had been her first and only boyfriend, but she was so young. And now he was suddenly back standing in front of her again…

James and Betty got to talking. It was like no time had passed. He seemed interested in what Betty was studying at NYU. His initial gap year had turned into three years, but he was planning on going to school in the city starting next fall. He wanted to know all about university and what it was like. He wanted to study business and acting. Betty felt the need to impress James and make school seem like it was the best thing that ever happened to her.

After she got back from dinner, Betty couldn't tell if she was elated or still in shock. She always thought about what it would be like to run into James, but when it finally happened it felt kind of disappointing.

Betty's phone dinged with a text - it was James.

Hey kid.

Her face burned but she couldn't help but break out into a smile. That familiar sadness she usually had when her birthday was over didn't arrive this time, Instead, there was a different feeling: a hopeful longing.

Chapter 3

The Great War

     Marjorie stood on the edge of the boardwalk waiting for John's army ship to dock. Her eyes became transfixed by a large bird flying high above in the distance, as though it was watching the crowd beneath its wings on the ship dock below. The sky over the horizon had the pinkish hue of a beautiful sunset over the Statue of Liberty away in the distance. Marjorie appreciated the crisp fresh air of autumn as she inhaled a cool breath. The exhale looked like smoke blowing out of her mouth. John was coming home to New York today, and he had made it through the horrors of World War 2 alive…

     This moment was the one thing she had been longing to have for so long. She was so grateful John had survived the war. She loved him so much and wanted to marry him and have his children. It was no secret. They were best friends, a partnership. It was love.

Marjorie had kept every letter John wrote to her throughout the war. His words got stronger with love throughout the war - but near the end, she felt the tone in his letters change. John didn't think he was going to make it out of the war alive. He had started writing letters of love and goodbyes to Marjorie.

Although John had made it out of the war in one piece, he was not coming home the same man anymore. His body had been battered and bruised. His feet hurt. His eyes were darkened, his skin looked dull, and the whites of his eyes a foggy pink. John hadn't slept in a very long time. Every time he closed his eyes to sleep, he heard the bombs, the gunshots, and the screams of men. Worst of all, he continued to hear the final screams and breaths of his good friend, Jack.

Marjorie had no idea yet just how different John had become from what he had seen and felt. Life would never be the same for him. The trauma he had endured was simply unimaginable.

He stood on the wooden platform and looked at Marjorie, smiling. She ran over to him and he wrapped his arms around her, holding her tight. The two held each other for a very long time, her head in his chest, listening to his heartbeat. She had dreamed of this moment since the moment John had left.

When Marjorie finally let go of John's embrace, it was clear that something had changed in him when she looked into his eyes. They were a different blue color than Marjorie had remembered. The hug had been long but it wasn't the warm embrace Marjorie had envisioned it to be for the last two years. For the first time, it dawned on Marjorie just how difficult this was going to be. She hugged John again and held him tight for even longer this time. She smelled his jacket and it smelled terrible. It stunk of dirt, blood, vomit, and body odor. His figure was much bonier than when he had left. He seemed to be more of a ghost of the man who she remembered and had daydreamed about the whole time he had been gone.

Marjorie peered out at the other soldiers scattered around the dock. Many didn't have anyone, and that made Marjorie sad to see. The electricity of the crowd waiting felt different now than just moments earlier, the excitement had turned to painful relief. The soldiers had come home hardened men who had seen too much for one lifetime.

While Marjorie held her man tight, he had never felt further away from her. It was as though John was trapped behind a blood-stained-glass window. Marjorie vowed to herself that she would always be his, but she knew that they were nowhere close to being out of the woods yet.

John stood in shock that he was here at this moment because when he closed his eyes, the color of crimson clover red cast the shadows of blood.

He only saw one thing - Jack.

Chapter 4

Back To December

Betty fell fast and hard back in love with James. They had been hanging out every night after James finished his shift at work around 8 - he would come to pick her up in his Chevy truck and they would go for a drive. They hadn't officially talked about it yet, but they were a couple again in Betty's eyes. They would make out in their favorite spot overlooking the twinkling lights of the town. They spent every day together during the winter break. A lot of it just involved snuggling on the couch and watching a movie. Sometimes he would stay late and ended up sleeping over at her house. She didn't want her mom to know, so he would quietly leave early in the morning before she got up. He made Betty feel so happy, and she had started to dread the end of winter break and having to go back to school.

"You are so smart Betty. I feel like I can really talk to you. I'm so glad we reconnected."

James was sound asleep next to a very awake Betty. He had a sharp jawline and there was something about James' expression where he always looked a little unimpressed. His eyebrows sank to the middle above the ridge of his nose, permanently wrinkled like that from him making that face too often. Even when he was sleeping, James looked effortlessly cool. His brow relaxed a little, but he still had that same impartial look to him. Betty's mom had told her that James looked like James Dean. Betty wasn't sure who that was, and her mom explained he was the most handsome actor of his time, back in a different era.

She noticed his phone light up. She knew it was wrong but she couldn't resist the temptation to look. Who would be texting him at 1 am? She snuck over and looked at his screen. The name was Ally. Betty's face burned. She couldn't open the text because she didn't know the passcode. She knew who Ally was though - she was James' ex-fling from last August. Judging by her texting him so late, she could tell that it was probably something that they both wouldn't want Betty to see.

Betty couldn't sleep for a while after that. She stared at James next to her who was still passed out soundly, looking like he had no care in the world. She had been burned by him before…but that was so long ago, and they were older now. She felt jealous at the thought of James being with Ally this past summer. He had assured her that they were over - that he didn't love her or even think about her anymore. But something deep down in Betty's gut was telling her that there was much more to this story than James had been letting on. She saw that there was something in James' eyes when he had talked about her to Betty and told her what had happened. They had spent the entire summer together. She had seen pictures of them together online and they had looked so happy together. James had looked at Ally the same way that Betty looked at James. He seemed to be reaching for her. She even looked effortlessly cooler than James, and that was saying a lot.

The next morning Betty poked him early to wake him up.
"Oh yeah hey I forgot… will you come with me to my friend's New Year's party this weekend?" he asked her while still half asleep.
"Yes of course!" Betty answered without hesitation.

The NYE party was at James' friend's apartment in Brooklyn. Everyone there was 3 or 4 years older than Betty and the minute she arrived she instantly felt out of place and awkward. Her New Year's party outfit felt silly and trashy compared to the other girls' nice black and blue midi dresses and nice jewelry. Betty was familiar with feeling out of place, but it made her feel worse that James suddenly felt like a different person around his friends. Betty had a feeling and sensed that they had already talked amongst each other about how young James' new "fling" was. It made Betty feel sad and disappointed. She had high hopes that his friends would welcome her with open arms and accept her as one of their own. And yet, it felt like there was a wall between her and the rest of the group. Betty was on the outside of their inside joke. She became reserved and quiet, smiling and nodding but didn't want to offer her own words unless asked a question.

During dinner with everyone at the table, Betty put her hand on James' hand. She didn't do it on purpose, it just happened. James pulled away, and he didn't seem to even notice her sitting next to him. He was deep in conversation with his friend. It was so embarrassing for Betty and she wished she hadn't tried to touch him like a girlfriend would. She felt like everyone at the table noticed him rejecting her, except for James himself. She began to realize that she felt like only an accessory to James at this party - she was just there along for the ride. He seemed to not notice at all that she had been sitting there quietly while conversations flowed naturally around her, everyone talking to someone about something, except for Betty who was nursing her drink quietly.

James went for a smoke outside at the party around 11:30. He didn't come back for 20 minutes, and Betty sat alone on the couch while everyone else was laughing in the kitchen. She didn't feel welcome there. She was mad at James and didn't want to sit there anymore. She had a feeling James had lost track of time and didn't care that much about doing the countdown to midnight with her. He was too busy with his guy friends and he obviously wasn't concerned about her being left alone inside.

Betty couldn't stand another minute of this torture and decided to leave the party. Mostly because she was mad, and also because she could feel herself about to start crying, and the thought of James' friends seeing her this way was too embarrassing to bear.

She grabbed her coat and ran out the door before anyone noticed. She missed the midnight countdown, and Betty knew James didn't even notice she was gone because he didn't bother to text her until well after the countdown around 12:30.

As Betty rode the train back home feeling alone and disheartened, she watched as the drunken crowds of friends all laughed together. She held back her tears, too embarrassed to show anyone she might be upset on a night when everyone was supposed to be happy. She regretted ever getting back together with James, she knew this feeling all too well…

Betty and James had a huge blow-up fight through text into and through the next day. Betty couldn't control her emotions. She felt livid at James' inability to feel any empathy or sympathy about how she might feel meeting and being around all his friends who clearly hadn't been very accepting of her at all. He seemed incapable of putting himself in Betty's shoes.

"It was no big deal," he spouted out. "Why are you being sooo pissy? You could have just come outside and gotten me." Then he told her that his friends thought it was kind of weird that she had just disappeared. He scolded her like a child about how he was so worried about her and it ruined the rest of his night and his entire New Year' Eve.

Betty was blind with rejection and rage at his feeble inability to understand. Her feelings were so hurt. How was he turning this around into *him* having his night ruined? It killed her to think of all his friends probably talking about her negatively after she had left. Once again, she had been hurt by James. She was angry at herself for falling into his web and trap again. Like a black widow getting caught in her own web. She should have known better, she thought to herself.

The text that had popped up on James' phone last week shook Betty inside. Everything started to feel even more twisted and bitter in the light of the morning. Her anger wouldn't subside. She wanted to go back to the beginning of December when things were so much simpler. She wanted to go back to just yesterday when she was listening to James laughing on the way to the party, squeezing her hand in the back of the taxi.

It was New Year's Day, but it didn't feel like a refresh or a new start. It felt like there was now a dark shadow haunting her into the new calendar

year, and James once again began to feel like a
stranger.

<u>Chapter 5</u>

The Prophecy

Alison peeked around the corner and down the stairway of the hotel, and she could see half of the lobby and bar. Lucy and August were standing together and appeared to be having a serious conversation. Alison watched as they talked to each other, trying to figure out what it was about. He rubbed her stomach and then kissed Lucy, and it was the first time Alison had seen them really be affectionate with each other.

August had told Alison that Lucy barely touched him anymore and that he thought they were as good as over. He seemed so sincere that Alison didn't have a choice but to believe him. Why would he lie to her?

She decided she needed a break from the hotel… She had the whole day to kill and decided to take a walk around Coney Island.

She sat on a bench, staring out at the ocean. She could hear her father's voice in her head. Her father was as cold as ice.

"*You are not right in the head child*!" he had said to her the night before she ran. In retaliation, Alison had spread hundreds of papers all around her room and trashed his office and his folders of important documents and threw them around angrily and haphazardly. Alison relished the thought of her dad realizing what she had done and finding the mess she had left. It was revenge for the plans they had made with the doctor. She had also stolen his typewriter and taken it with her.

Alison kept walking along on the boardwalk. She felt someone's eyes staring at her. She came across an old lady sitting still on a bench, gazing at Alison. She was wearing a tattered green dress and was cradling an orange orb. The strange lady appeared wise, but Alison had a hard time knowing how trustworthy she really seemed.

"Would you like a reading, Miss?"

Alison was about to keep walking, but something told her to stop. She remembered she had left one last coin in her pocket from her tips the night before.

Alison sat down on the bench with the psychic. She took Alison's hand and held it tight.

"A writer!" She exclaimed.

"Kind of…" Alison replied.

"And a musician!" the lady retorted.

She stared at Alison's face,
pausing. "Someone has wronged you. Someone close to you. Your mother or father, perhaps."

Alison didn't reply. She didn't want to give up any information about herself, in case they were looking for her.

The old lady held Alison's hand tight as she closed her eyes. She stayed silent for what felt like forever to Alison. It made her nervous. What could she tell about her?

"You have been playing with fire…" The lady said in a different and more sinister tone than she had begun with.

"I see a child… and a man. And there is a prophecy of an invisible string of consequences which I cannot see yet… You are in terrible danger! You need to run… my child."

Alison pulled her hand away and quickly stood up from the bench, a little bewildered. This was not the way her reading was supposed to go. She stood in disbelief at the stark change in tone. Alison did not consider herself to be a child - she was seventeen, after all. Alison ran away feeling scared and with goosebumps.

Later that night after Alison had finished singing, August held Alison in his arms on the terrace of the hotel. He kissed her and they slowly danced together in the darkness and quiet of the night. The heat of the day had cooled, and the breeze felt so good. The moon was full and bright.

Alison shuddered on the inside at the memory of the psychic's reading that morning. What had she meant by an invisible string? She loved August and didn't want to run from him.

August was quiet, perhaps he too was deep in thought about their relationship and the future? Alison secretly made a wish, begging to be allowed to stay in the arms of this man who made her feel so whole.

<u>Chapter 6</u>

Never Grow Up

Just as winter break had ended, Betty knew that she and James had probably ended too. Betty's mom dropped her off at the train station to go back to New York for the second semester. Betty went a couple of days early - she felt anxious about the start of her classes and wanted to make sure she was as prepared as she could be. She had some reading she needed to do and a book to get for her English class.

Betty dragged her suitcase down the sidewalks of the city. People on the street seemed unusually cranky and she felt like she was in everyone's way while lugging her huge and heavy suitcase across the broken pavement and ice. She wanted to yell at all of them that she lived here too! She wasn't a tourist with a suitcase, she was just going home like everyone else.

She dug her keys out of her bag and opened her dorm room. Inez wasn't coming home for a couple of days, so she had the place to herself. Betty didn't like the room without Inez to fill it with her laughter and excitement. It felt cold, dark, and empty when she walked in. Water from the raindrops dripped down on the outside of her dorm windows. The Christmas lights they had put up last month now looked sad and deflated in the wet melted snow of January. It reminded Betty of a happier and more mysterious time before James had crept his way back into her life. She had a flashback to James dropping her hand on New Year's, how she couldn't find him for the countdown. How her countdown to midnight was spent crying on the train home, alone. It all seemed so dumb in the light of day, yet trying to brush it all aside didn't seem to ease the sting. Fresh tears were on the horizon of Betty's eyes, and she had been holding them back all day in fear that once she started, there would be no end in sight for at least a couple of days. She didn't want Inez to see her like that. She wanted to seem like she had an amazing break and New Year.

Betty lay on her bed. The dorm building was still quiet. Most people would return tomorrow or the next day and Betty wondered if she was the only one in the whole building tonight. She pictured her mom's fireplace in their living room, how she was just there this morning, drinking coffee. Now the quiet of the building and the dorm furniture felt so fake and uncomfortable. Temporary. It didn't feel like home at all.

Pulling her blanket up over her neck and head, Betty closed her eyes and imagined she was still back in her room at home. She wished she had never grown up, and she longed to know the comfortable feeling of laying down in her mother's bed. Adulthood felt uncomfortable and scary. Finally, she allowed her emotions to unload, and it felt like a volcano erupting onto her pillow, her tears ricocheting down her cheeks and onto her bed sheets.

Clothes were scattered all over the floor of Betty's half of the room. She and Inez were a messy combination - their space was never clean. Betty looked under her bed. There was a pile of clothes spilling out from her unpacked suitcase poking out from under Betty's bed. Some tights, a t-shirt, and her favorite cardigan. She pulled it out and shook off the dust and hair stuck to it. It reminded her of James and suddenly had a thought of setting the cardigan on fire just to watch it burn.

Two days later, James showed up at Betty's dorm to apologize. He knew he had been in the wrong, and tried his best to make it up to Betty.

Inez had already heard all about James and everything that had happened over the break. She was not impressed when she met him and it was a bit awkward. Inez felt very protective of Betty and was quietly hostile towards James.

James invited Betty upstate to Connecticut the next weekend to where his parents had moved to. They were suddenly right back in love, and it was as though the huge fight had never happened. It was winter, but somehow the weather was crisp and fall-like, with the sun shining on leaves that had held on tight to the trees.

Betty met James' parents and they showed him old photo albums from when he was a little kid. He was so cute wearing glasses and Betty secretly thought about how cute their kids would be. James had a warm and loving family, and seeing the twin-size bed he had grown up in made Betty love him even more. James was so embarrassed every time his mom said anything about James being a kid. It was nice to see him vulnerable for a change, it was a side of James she had never really seen before. She felt so grateful to have been welcomed into his family so easily, and it had seemed to make up for the terrible first meeting with James' friends.

As they drove back to the city, Betty felt happy and relaxed. She looked over at James driving, and he was gorgeous. They sang together and time seemed to stop as they took the scenic routes. James didn't live in the city but promised to visit Betty every weekend at school.

Betty spent her time during the week looking forward to his visit. Things had become so much brighter this semester, but Betty was still battling the doubt within herself and her confidence at school.

Her anxiety followed her around campus like a dark cloud leashed to her.

Chapter 7

Peace

John lay beside Marjorie and listened to her slowly breathing as she slept so soundly. The memories of his time in the war continued to haunt him every night, and he found himself envious of Marjorie's ability to close her eyes and not see the same things that he would see. Flashbacks and nightmares created turmoil, leaving him reeling and agitated. Marjorie always found a way to calm him back down, but in the morning, he always awoke with the same sense of dread, paralyzed and anxious.

The horrible last moments of the day Jack died hadn't stopped haunting John. Jack was John's best friend and they had become close during training as medics together. They were inseparable.

The memory played over and over of the day Jack died. John attempted to peel his eyes open - but the dust and sand hardened his eyelashes shut. It was June 6th, 1944 - D-Day, and he and Jack were in battle huddled on the beach in fetal position. Suddenly there was an explosion, deafening John and blinding him with dirt and sand. The sand was up his nose and he coughed some up too. His mouth had never felt drier and stuck like glue. John and Jack were trapped in a collapsed dugout, covered in debris, mud, and the smell of blood. The sand was saturated with blood, and John feared the worst.

When he was finally able to open his eyes, Jack lay beside him - silent. John looked at Jack's lifeless body and felt pure agony. He pulled himself over as much as he could under the rubble and reached his arm out to Jack's neck.
 He yelled to his commander who was also with them.

"I think he's bleeding out!" John screamed.

There was no heartbeat on Jack and John couldn't believe this was happening. John felt in that moment as though he had watched Jack fall off the earth and fall away outwards, reaching out to grasp his hand and pull him back down, but there was no coming back from death. Death is final.

John didn't know exactly when Jack had passed, but it must have been sudden. Jack had been hit in the head by flying debris. John couldn't do the one thing he had come to war to do, to save soldiers. He had been hit too and was still lying trapped under debris.

Jack was stiff, still and cold when John checked his heartbeat again. John lay where he was and wept. He reached into Jack's pocket and took out the small book Jack loved and had kept on him at all times. He didn't have time to think before more shots started firing over the hill onto the beach. Screams of men echoed across the landscape as John felt chilled to the bone. He held Jack's book tightly in his hands and passed out, the echoes of screams in the distance fading with his consciousness as the world started to turn dark…

When John woke up the next day he was being pulled up by fellow American soldiers. It was a completely different day - the bombs had stopped, the rain had ended, and even the sun had come out.

John sat in the medical tent in complete shock and disbelief. Rumors among the nurses and soldiers were that the war was ending. John thought of seeing Marjorie again and was full of longing, but still couldn't believe that Jack would not be going home too…

The little book in John's pocket poked him from the inside. He pulled it out and opened it up, curious of the words written inside this tiny book. It was a frayed bound book of poems, simply titled "The Manuscript". There was no author written on it. John opened up the small and old tattered page of the cover. Inside he read a small inscription in beautiful handwriting. It wrote:

Dear Jack,

I love you, it's ruining my life…

but I hope I get to love you in the next life too.

Love, Your Augustina

This part of the war was not covered in medical school or soldier training. The loss of his friend and the thought of Jack's wife Augustina and son living without him overwhelmed John. He didn't know how he would ever speak about Jack to anyone, even to Marjorie. He felt like a failure in that he couldn't protect his best friend - the loss felt unbearable and surreal.

Marjorie looked so sweet sleeping now, and John felt sad at the thought he would never be able to bring her true peace again after what he had been through. Life would never truly feel good for him, and he knew that would hurt Marjorie.
John got out of bed and took a look through Jack's tiny book again. He became engrossed by all the little poems scattered within it. The book was almost falling apart, probably mostly from being in Jack's pocket throughout the war.
John wondered who had written the poems. How did Augustina get this book and how much must it

have meant to her? He knew had to return it to her but was dreading the thought of it. He didn't know how he was going to face the woman Jack had loved so much. The woman whom Jack constantly spoke about, the woman whose heart must have been shattered when she found out Jack had died. John thought about just mailing the book to Augustina but felt like that would be too cowardly.

He found Marjorie's book tape and started taping the fallen-out pages back in. He couldn't return it to Jack's wife in such a poor state.

If he could do anything for Jack now, it would be to bring back this small form of peace to Augustina.

Chapter 8

Peter

Peter had liked Betty since the moment he saw her on the first day she had moved in with Inez. He and his girlfriend were still together, but it was not going well. Peter had put Betty into his mind's pile of Inez's friends - off-limits and not to be messed with, but he just couldn't get Betty out of his mind. He found himself constantly thinking about her. He would make up excuses to go see Inez, just to see Betty too. He tried not to make it seem too obvious. He loved going to hang out with the girls on Fridays. Peter thought Betty was sweet and kind, talented and smart. He loved how passionate she was when she talked about music and books. He loved her laugh and how she would tilt her head back without worry when she chuckled. He loved how her nose would wrinkle up.

So, on the night of Betty's birthday eve, Peter decided to break up with his girlfriend. It was the right thing to do because he knew his feelings for

Betty were stronger. He wanted to be with Betty, yet he wasn't in the right place to tell her, especially Inez. He was worried what Inez would think, that it might create a weird dynamic between the girls.

Peter arrived at the entrance of Betty and Inez's building, excited to see Betty again after the long holiday break. But before he could even enter the building, he saw Betty leaving with a guy he didn't recognize, and he turned around to hide before she could see him. "Who…" he thought to himself, dazed and confused. He was crushed to learn of Betty's new relationship that had started so suddenly over the break.

Betty was taking a new Writing 100 course this semester and it had quickly become her favorite class. The professor was wise and had a lot of interesting ideas to share about writing. The class was huge and taught in a lecture style, so the professor didn't know many students' names. He had no idea who Betty was, since the class was chock-full of freshman students and the lecture hall was so immense. Betty always sat near the back of class, she liked to disappear into the crowd. University had been the opposite of high school in the sense that depending on the size of the class, Betty could blend into the mass of other students and no teacher would really single her out or even know her name all semester.

"Write what you know." That was the theme of this professor's fiction writing course. He was a

published novelist who now taught at NYU for kicks. Betty had never read or heard of the books the professor had written but that didn't matter. He was good at talking about writing and inspired Betty. She watched his beard flop up and down, he looked a little like Santa Clause and gave off a similar energy. You could tell he loved his job. Up until this class, Betty had only really considered poems and songwriting, but this professor made her interested in writing fiction stories.

Betty's confidence when it came to writing was at an all-time low and she wasn't used to having to submit a finished product to judgmental classmates. It felt unnatural to share such personal things with strangers. She had to write and trade work with other students, and then they would meet and critique. It was nerve-wracking. Betty had started to question whether she should drop the course altogether.

Then Peter walked into the classroom. Betty looked up and felt a rush of happiness to see his familiar face. He saw her, grinned, and came over to sit right next to her.

"I meant to text you to ask about this class. Inez told me you were taking it and I'm short 3 credits, so I thought I'd take it with you!" He told Betty excitedly.

The two friends sat together every Monday and Wednesday for the lectures and workshops. Betty looked forward to the class all week. The two would crack jokes and quietly giggle as they sat together in class.

One time, Peter playfully took one of Betty's rings off her middle finger and placed it on her ring finger.

"That looks good on you!" He joked. Betty died inside. Peter didn't realize just how much that silly joke meant to her. Peter knew about James but pretended as though he didn't exist. They bordered on flirting and friendship - a line that was frequently crossed back and forth. Sometimes Betty felt like Peter could read her mind, but on other days it was clear he had no idea the feelings Betty was starting to have for him.

Betty didn't want to drudge up any jealousy and give James a reason to bolt. She felt as though she was always walking on eggshells with him. She decided not to mention to James that Peter was in a class with her. It felt like a small white lie and she didn't want him to know about their blossoming friendship.

Poor Inez had to hear a lot about James that semester. Betty was constantly on the ins and outs with him. She never knew whether it would be a good day or a bad day in their relationship. James was either attentive and loving to Betty, or suddenly without warning cold and distant. Betty was worried he still talked to Ally once in a while, but now she didn't know if she even deserved to be mad at him, considering she constantly talked to Peter, even though she felt like it was mostly about school and writing stuff.

One of Betty's biggest fears was allowing her parents' failed marriage to define her. She didn't want to feel cursed in her relationships because of her mom and dad's inability to stick to their own relationship. She didn't understand how her dad had given up on her mom so easily - it was a question that had taunted her for years.

It sounded cliché, but James reminded Betty of her dad. Maybe it was his nonchalant attitude or the lack of empathy James displayed while they fought, but Betty was starting to realize they were weirdly similar. James and her dad had a familiar pessimism about the world around them.

Peter was the opposite. He was sunshine, so full of optimism. He always saw the good side and loved everything about everyone. Everything he touched became full of light and happiness.

One Friday night, Peter came over to the girls' place. After a blur of red wine-induced dancing in the dorm room and an adventure through the city, Betty found herself exasperated with happiness. Her cheeks ached from smiling and laughing all night with Inez and Peter. They had been hanging out every day. The sky above was a deep red hue, almost as dark as maroon.

They woke up the next morning a little hungover, but full of memories from the night before.

"How'd we end up on the floor?" Betty laughed as she asked Peter and Inez.

Later that day, Betty decided to talk to Inez more about her crush on Peter and her doubts about James. Betty already knew how Inez felt about James. Inez thought James didn't treat Betty well enough.

"I know I don't know much about relationships, but I don't think it's supposed to be this hard. You're not supposed to feel scared every day." Inez said in a tone that made Betty feel a bit stupid. She knew her relationship with James was not stable, but she felt trapped because she truly believed she was in love with him.

"My psychology profession put forth a theory that there is no such thing as bad thoughts - only your actions talk. I liked it. I say go ahead and think about Peter all you want! Just don't tell me anything gross…he is my brother after all."

Betty thought about what Inez said. She was right, what was the harm in having some thoughts about Peter? It wasn't like she was cheating on James unless she acted on it, right? Was it still high infidelity if she never actually did anything about her crush on Peter?

Deep down Betty knew the truth.

<u>Chapter 9</u>

Fortnight

Alison couldn't tell you exactly when her intrusive thoughts got stronger, but she couldn't stop picturing the Albatross Hotel going up in flames.

The building looked as though it was made of dry wooded kindling, just waiting and begging for someone to light a match and burn it down. It almost appeared as though it was built to someday be lit on fire. She knew she would never actually do it, but thinking about it made her feel out of control like she wasn't herself. She felt like she was someone else when she would think of those things. She had shared some intrusive thoughts with her doctor once, and that was when he had probably told Alison's parents that he believed she was insane and needed "fixing."

Lucy's eyes glared towards Alison from across the lobby into the restaurant. Lucy knew the moment she saw Alison that she would be a

problem. She knew her husband, and the way
Alison looked at August was crystal clear to
Lucy. August was well-meaning but was weak when
it came to women. It was how the relationship
between August and Lucy had begun - in secret.

It would be the thirteenth night of the affair
and August had started to become very
nervous. He was worried Lucy was becoming
suspicious. August sensed something was wrong
with Lucy. Her demeanor was distant and she was
staying up later than usual. Her pregnancy had
rendered her tired early on in the evening, and she
usually went to bed early.

Before Alison went to play her music that
night, Lucy stopped Alison on the stairwell, her
pregnant belly looking larger than the day before.
Her swollen feet ached with every step she took.

"You are not the exception." Lucy sharply
said, staring at Alison. "You think you know him,
but you don't. He won't pick you. You are the fruit
that spoils, and he won't help but move on. You will
be forgotten."

Alison was floored and didn't know what to
say. Her throat closed in shock at Lucy even
speaking to her. She fled up the stairs, embarrassed
and in disbelief that Lucy had implied that she knew
what had been going on between her and August.

Later that night, Alison was playing her
piano songs, holding back her true emotions.
August pulled Alison aside into his office during her
break. He wanted to tell her that it was over

between them. The whiskey on his breath and the tobacco smoke suffocating the air only made his words feel more intrusive. He grabbed her by the strap of her dress and pulled her down onto a chair. He loved her but wasn't ready to give up his family for her.

"I can't do this anymore. We have to stop. No more."

Alison looked up at his face with sadness and disbelief. She really thought he loved her back. She truly thought that they were soul mates.

"Alison, look into my eyes. It's the last time you will ever see them." August had told Alison those hurtful words, and they echoed back to her. "Tonight is your last performance - You have to leave the hotel tomorrow. I'm sorry. Goodbye, Alison."

Alison started to crouch down as she held back the tears. The tone within his words felt so harsh and scolding - like she was a child and he was the father. The torrid affair was over, and all that was left was Allison's souvenir of a broken heart. August felt he was doing Alison a favor, he had to scare her away. He needed to put her in her place, he had allowed her to become too comfortable with him.

She bolted to her room and didn't finish the night's performance - August was a fool for thinking she would go back and sing after he tore her heart open. He was a coward, disguised with a lion's roar.

A distraught Alison sat on her bed, tears streaming down her face. She knew it was insane, but she fantasized about jumping off the top of the hotel, just to see August come running to help her afterwards. She wanted him to know what it might feel like to actually lose her. Alison was good at coming up with ridiculous thoughts she would never actually act on, but she had learned her lesson never to share these thoughts with anyone. That was how she had gotten into this situation in the first place.

One intrusive thought morphed into the next. She was staring at the box of matches on the desk...

"How did it end?" The people of Coney Island would ask about the infamous hotel's demise for years to come. Alison played that scene over and over again in her head, like a montage in an old silent movie. People would hear all about the flames that burned *"The Lover House"* down to the ground… karma for August's quiet treason against her.

<u>Chapter 10</u>

Coney Island

John stood on the sidewalk at the steps of Jack's old home address on Coney Island - staring at the crumpled piece of paper with the street number in his shaking hands. He had taken two trains and walked around for half an hour looking for the right street until he finally found Jack's house.

There were toys scattered across the front lawn of the small house. He took a deep breath and stood at the entrance of the gate to the walkway. When he knocked on the door he heard tiny little feet run and open the door.

"Mommy! A soldier is here!" The little boy left the door cracked open and ran away.

John was wearing his army uniform. He wanted to deliver Jack's poetry book to Augustina personally while looking official and professional. She would have already had the formal letter and then had Jack's army tag and other belongings brought to her.

Augustina had not been expecting John, and so when she opened the door, she stared at him in confusion. He took his hat off.

"Augustina?" he asked.

"Yes?" she said.

"I'm John."

"Oh!" Augustina paused and then pulled John in for a hug. It was clear that Jack had written to her about him.

The two lingered in an awkward silence after the hug ended. Both didn't know what to say to each other.

"I…I have something for you." John stammered as he pulled out Jack's book and handed it to her.

"Oh my goodness! Thank you." Augustina looked down at the book and stared at it. She didn't say anything else for a long time. Her eyes were welling up but she was trying to hide it.

"Please, come in."

"Oh no, that's alright. I came unannounced. I just wanted to make sure this got back to you." He hesitated.

"You must. You can't just leave me here in tears. You must tell me all about Jack and what happened in the war. Please-" She was trying not to appear begging, but he couldn't just leave.
John wasn't about to argue with his friend's widowed wife. He came inside the front door and took his boots off. The little boy came up to him

and handed him a cookie. It was Jack's son and John saw his eyes in him right away.

There was a picture of Jack holding a guitar on the wall behind Augustina. John's eyes were drawn to seeing his friend in a happy time other than war. He looked different and peaceful. It was a version of Jack that John had never had the chance to know.

Augustina brought John a cup of tea and sat down. She seemed frazzled and nervous to have the familiar stranger as a guest. She didn't know what to say or where to begin. John nervously thanked her for her hospitality.

Augustina replied, "My parents both worked in the hotel industry, so I pride myself on my hosting skills."

"Jack told me all about you, so I feel like we already know each other," John said.

"Did he tell you about the huge fight we had before he left? Our love was calamitous at times, but we really loved each other…" Augustina trailed off and was staring awkwardly at her son's toys on the floor.

John could feel the insurmountable grief on Augustina's shoulders. He felt the urge to pull her into her arms and hold her, and so without thinking, he did just that. He held her tight in his arms, just like he had held Marjorie so many times before. She cried in his arms and he just held her for he wasn't sure how long. The little boy didn't seem to mind the strange man holding his mother, but he was concerned about why she was so sad. The small audible sobs of Augustina ended.

"I'm so sorry, I snotted all over your coat."

"Don't worry about it." They both chuckled and it felt nice to laugh together. John felt like he had known Augustina for a long time. Maybe because Jack had talked about her so much.

"Here… I want you to have this..." Augustina went into the front closet and brought out an old guitar case - "It used to be mine but I had given it to Jack. He was the musical one. I would write the lyrics, but I struggled with the tunes. That's where Jack excelled. That's how we met. We wrote some great songs together. He was my muse…" Augustina sighed.

John could see the memories of Jack written all over her face. "He told me."

He sat staring at Agustina and felt obligated to do his best to take her pain away.

"Jack told me all about you every day. It feels like I already know you. You were all he talked about." John laughed.

"He wrote to me about you, but I never thought we would be meeting like this. Thank you for coming and bringing me my beloved little book back." Augustina was sincere with her words.

Without thinking, John leaned in and kissed Augustina on the cheek. He wanted to make sure she was going to be okay when he left, even though he could tell she was in pain.

"Do you? …. Augustina trailed off. "Never mind. It's stupid."

"Do I what? Tell me."

"Do you…want to come to Coney Island with us right now? We were about to leave right before you showed up. It's where Jack and I met, so I like to go there often."

"I'd love to." John hadn't forgotten that he had dinner plans with Marjorie, but he felt like this was more important. She would understand when he told her where he had been.

The two newly acquainted friends followed Augustina's son down the street toward the center of Coney Island and the boardwalk. John felt at ease in the presence of Augustina - she made him feel like they were the only two people in the world. Augustina sat down on a bench. John and Jack Jr ran out to play in the sand. The sun was going down and it was becoming darker and colder quickly. The lights of the Ferris wheel and the sounds of kids screaming filled the air. Augustina pictured Jack sitting next to her and wondered what he would be saying if he were here. What jokes would he have made? What food would he have ordered for him and Jack Jr to share? Augustina felt as though her soul had been split in half when she learned of Jack's death.

"You're the love of my life." he would say quietly to her, so many times before he left for the war.

Now Augustina sat in disbelief of his passing, yearning and aching to feel his embrace just once more. She stared up at the terrace of the hotel building where they had first met. She pictured them up there years ago, young and naïve of what was to come. It was the place where they first danced together. She had worn a red dress that night, with matching red lipstick. Now all Augustina could picture up there were phantoms of the past, and she wondered what they would think if they saw her now, barely being able to get out of bed to take care of Jack Jr.

Jack was the loss of her life.

Over the next few months, John would visit Augustina and Jack Jr on Coney Island every couple of weeks. He never told Marjorie about the visits. It wasn't that he wanted to be secretive about it, he just thought that she might not fully understand why he continued to see Augustina even after returning Jack's book. He felt guilty for lying to Marjorie about his whereabouts but continued to do it anyway. He wasn't sure why he wasn't being truthful with Marjorie, since he had always been faithful to her.

With every visit, Augustina and John grew closer. It was a new friendship that they both needed to help heal from the loss of Jack. John never felt anything more than friendship for Augustina. He could never cross that line with Jack's wife, even if he was no longer here. But sometimes he caught Augustina gazing at him, and he wasn't sure if she just looked at everyone that way. There was a longing in her eyes that he couldn't shake, but John loved to make her laugh. It was something he hadn't seen the first couple of times they had met, and now it had become a regular occurrence. She deserved to laugh after everything she had been through. Spending time with Augustina made John feel closer to Jack again. He didn't have to grieve alone when he was with her, and neither did she. Their friendship made sense, but John sensed it was beginning to mean something more between them. He knew their time together was running out.

Marjorie and John's relationship had been so different ever since his return home from the war. Marjorie found herself constantly sitting back at home in her living room alone thinking about him and what she could do to help bring him back to who he was before he left. She felt a constant sting of sadness. She knew the truth just by looking into John's eyes. He had something to hide, but she couldn't figure out what was going on with him.

John's guitar case was sitting by the front door and Marjorie suddenly had the urge to look through it. He was hiding something and she needed to find out what it was. On a hunch, she opened up the case and searched it thoroughly, and sure enough, she found a letter:

Dear John,

Marjorie stared at the words in disbelief. She knew the pulse on her and John's relationship had felt strained and weak - now she knew why. He was tormented by love. A triangle of deceit and broken hearts. Marjorie loved John enough to tolerate a friendship between Augustina and him, but now Augustina had crossed a line. It was clear Augustina had no intention to act on her love for John, but it still felt like an invasion. The two had been playing with fire this whole time.

That night, Marjorie set the table with the fancy silverware and crystal glasses. She wanted to see that John loved her enough to move forward with their lives together. She felt as though he had only been tolerating her since the war. He had been distant and distracted. She felt bruised and torn.

Marjorie started to cry when he walked in the door. She was holding the letter.

"I love you, John."

John felt terrible for lying to Marjorie about his friendship with Augustina. It was a mistake to lie to her from the beginning. He never meant to hurt her. As the two sat holding each other in their living room, it dawned on both of them just what they had been through in the last few years. The war took everything from them and left them in ruins. It was up to them to rebuild from the ashes.

John had been planning this for weeks but suddenly felt that this moment was the right time. He got down on one knee and asked Marjorie to marry him.

"I talked to your dad..." John told her, full of hope.

Marjorie was in shock. John clearly loved her, and she felt a little embarrassed for ever thinking otherwise.

Together, they had survived the great war.

Chapter 11

The Bolter

When Betty was six years old, her dad hit black ice while he was driving with her in his truck. The memory was embedded in Betty's mind, and she never forgot the feeling of the tires losing grip on the pavement while Betty and her dad were spinning, as he tried to keep them from hitting the pole on the right and the oncoming car on their left. Betty screamed as she felt like this was the end of her life. She always had a fear of ending up upside down in a pond or a lake while being trapped in a sinking car, and now her fear was becoming a reality. The truck spun around two times and then slid down an embankment and landed on top of the frozen lake just below the road, cracking into the ice with shallow water below. Her dad moved quickly and calmly, making sure Betty undid her seatbelt as he grabbed her and pulled her onto his lap and then out of the driver's door. The shock of the cold water made her unaware of the blood from the cut she got from the broken ice and glass. She was wearing a blue dress that day, and the blood dripped over the front of it and onto the white snow as her dad carried her up to the side of the road. They both looked down at the truck sunk halfway under the water.

When it was all over, Betty felt a wave of relief, she couldn't believe she had made it through that alive. *It could have been so much worse,* her mom kept saying over and over again when she came to pick them up. Even though they had made it through mostly unharmed, the trust had been broken with her dad. Three years later, Betty's dad walked out on her and her mom and moved away to Florida with his new girlfriend. Grandma Marjorie nicknamed him "The Bolter". Betty didn't care for the nickname, so Marjorie never repeated it, but Betty did agree it was a fitting nickname for the man who had bolted on his family.

It was now springtime in New York City, and the winter had finally seemed to begin defrosting into a beautiful and crisp new season of chirping birds and sunshine.

Betty and James had been having fun together, and things were going well between them. She kept Peter and the creative writing course a secret from James. She knew he would get jealous, even though Peter was just her friend.

While walking back from class, Betty reflected on her first year away at school. She still felt like an imposter, and she still felt like she was faking it every day - but she realized how much she had grown, too. She was becoming more confident in her independence and was slowly gaining more courage. She had written a short story for class and read it aloud for the whole workshop. She had rehearsed in front of Inez and had been so nervous about it. Betty glowed with happiness hearing all of her classmates' positive comments about it. After that, she was writing more than she ever had. Something had been unlocked within her. She was now writing poems, song lyrics, short stories, and even thinking up ideas for a novel.

Sitting in front of her dorm room door, Betty found a small wrapped package and a bouquet of carnation flowers next to it. She opened it up to find a really old small book. She opened it up and there was an inscription on it.

It was obvious to Betty who it was from. Inside the front cover, there was writing signed, without a doubt, by the handwriting of a woman. She knew that Inez and Peter's Grandmother's name had been Augustina. Peter had used her name in one of the short stories he had written for class. Below Augustina's first inscription, there was another small piece of messy writing. She recognized the printing instantly.

Betty, I love you, it's ruining my life!

Betty felt her heart sink and soar at the same time. This was Peter's grand gesture that Inez had warned her about. It was the most romantic thing anyone had ever done for Betty. This was beyond what Betty had ever imagined. She instantly felt crushed by the weight of letting Peter down. Her peace had quickly turned into perplexion.

James did not need to know about the poetry book that Peter gave Betty, as it would give away that there might be something more than friendship between them. She didn't want James to know anything about Peter other than him being Inez's older brother.

Since Betty didn't want to seem guilty or like she had done anything wrong, she didn't bother to hide the book other than just placing it in the corner of her messy desk. She didn't think James would even notice it. This was a mistake and a naïve decision - because Inez was home when James came over and she recognized the book immediately. She didn't know it was a secret, and couldn't help but pick it up once she saw it on Betty's desk. Inez knew it well - she and Peter used to read through the poems as children at their grandmother's house. When Augustina died, it was one of the few things Peter wanted from his grandmother.

Once James caught on to where the book came from, the tone in the room changed. James hadn't seen the inscription. Inez was smart enough to hide that page. But the vibe suddenly felt stagnant and dimmed. James didn't want to be there anymore. It became awkward and quiet between James and Betty. He felt like ice.

"Peter is just like that, he thought I would like it… it's not a big deal!" Betty pleaded with James after he had gone quiet. Betty couldn't get James to smile or laugh like usual, and it made her feel angry and misunderstood. She felt like James was making a bigger deal out of Peter's gift of the book than it was. Then she remembered the night she saw the text from Ally on James' phone. The anger came out of her, raging through her throat, and turned into accusatory words.

"At least I don't text my exes like you do." The minute it came out of her mouth, Betty regretted saying anything about it. She knew that he hadn't done that since winter break, and she felt as if James had been loyal ever since. She wished she had never brought it up now, but it was too late.

"What are you even talking about?" James left her dorm hallway in a huff. She heard him muffle the word "Whore…" as he stormed away from her down the hall towards the stairs. Betty felt the same feeling of seething rage and misunderstanding that she had felt after their big fight on New Year's. She lay on her bed, feeling like a lovelorn schoolgirl - aching for her mistakes to be erased and rewound.

Inez came back into the room looking guilty. Betty sunk her face into her pillow and let out a muffled scream. She couldn't stand the feeling of fighting with James.

"I just can't decide between James and Peter. I love them both." Betty sighed. She had never been so open and vulnerable with Inez.

"Just, be careful with Peter. I don't want you to get hurt... Peter is lovely, but he can be trouble too. He's my brother and I love him, but I have seen a dark side of him you haven't Betty. I just want you to be careful."

Betty didn't know what Inez meant. Peter was perfect in Betty's eyes, she couldn't imagine him hurting her. If anything, Betty always felt like she was the one who might hurt Peter. The darkness in Peter was something that Betty couldn't see herself. She was blind to whatever it was Inez had been hinting at.

The tears wouldn't stop coming down on her pillow. Thankfully Inez was asleep now and didn't seem to notice the endless sniffling of Betty's nose. She didn't want to lose James or Peter, but she knew that she wasn't going to be able to keep both. She felt trapped in the middle. Losing either one of them was going to be equally heartbreaking.

Picturing James with other girls made her feel like she wanted to throw up. The idea of him getting back together with Ally made her feel sick and envious. She couldn't stand the idea of losing him, yet couldn't see herself losing Peter either. She didn't know what to do.

Here she had Peter, who was crazy for her. He was sweet, kind, funny, gentle, and safe. And then she had James - who left her feeling breathless.

James, who raised her heart rate with the sheer mention of his name. James, who she had spent years with since she was so young, languishing over, a little bit of an obsession. James, who had repeatedly hurt her. She realized no good could come of this situation. Either way, someone was going to get hurt, including Betty.

She checked James' location to see if she could see where he was. He had gone somewhere uptown, to a bar. She immediately regretted finding out where he was. Her imagination started to run wild in a chaotic mess of images in her mind of James drinking and laughing with other girls. She gave in an hour later and called him. His location was still at the bar and all she could imagine was him talking to other girls, and then going home with one. It started to drive her mental and she felt a hot anger and jealous rage steaming up inside of her.

His phone went straight to voicemail, and it made her feel like she had been stung with the same sharp pain of the ice from when her dad hit the back ice. She needed to escape, to get out of the city and clear her head. She felt overwhelmed with indecision and stress. She decided if there was ever a time to bolt, it was now.

As the fresh air hit her face on the sidewalk, she felt a sense of freedom. She had finally made her choice and it made her feel alive. She wanted to be with Peter.

Chapter 12

The Manuscript

Betty stepped off the train platform and started walking towards Coney Island. She hadn't been this far out of the city since her night in Brooklyn. It felt good to travel beyond the border of the university and the city to explore.

Peter had mentioned Coney Island multiple times, saying how much he loved it there as a kid. His grandmother used to take him and Inez there all the time when they were little kids. When Peter texted Betty back and asked if she would meet him there, Betty was already halfway to the subway station.

There was a bench overlooking the boardwalk and beach and Betty took a seat. She looked out over the horizon of the water. She heard an acoustic guitar playing in the distance. Trails of people kept walking by and interrupting the chords of the song, but Betty kept listening to it. She quickly realized that it was Peter playing. She got up and started walking towards the edge of the boardwalk and down the walkway. Peter had borrowed Betty's guitar the last time he was at her dorm. *"Your guitar has a special soul. I can't explain it, but it feels so good to play."*

Peter was full of light and happiness, and he didn't want Betty to know how nervous he had become the instant he heard Betty's voice from standing behind him.

Betty pulled out the old poetry book that Peter had given him. The two sat together on the bench. Reading the words of the book's poetry and goofily trying to place them into the melody of Peter's chords on the guitar. Their hips and arms cozied up together to stay warm. For the first time in a long time, Betty felt clarity. Peter felt like home, and she was ready to stay there. She longed to stay there, in a place she belonged.

The chords of Peter's guitar echoed across the waves of the ocean. They kept singing and turning the poetry into music late into the evening. People would walk by in the distance, enjoying the guitar from afar. It was everything Betty had ever wanted. Someone who enjoyed her company. Someone who she felt safe and relaxed with.

Later that night, when they got back to the city, they spent all night in Betty's room staying up late talking and laughing. Peter was letting his walls come down, and as Betty started to sense a little more about Peter's wild side, she wondered if that was what Inez was talking about when she said to be careful. Peter seemed to have secrets that Betty didn't know about. She could tell that he was hiding something under all that enthusiasm. Betty knew that he experimented with drugs but was starting to get a feeling that maybe it was more than that. She wasn't stupid. Peter seemed almost a little strung out on something. It worried Betty but she pushed the feeling aside.

Betty and Peter cuddled all night long, their hands and fingers intertwined. His hands were so soft and warm and she fit so perfectly lying with him. They fell asleep holding each other with his head on her neck. Betty felt like everything would be okay.

When Betty woke up, the night before felt like a dream and Betty quickly remembered the amazing time with Peter. When she opened her eyes, Peter was gone. She quickly checked her phone - no texts. No explanation. Betty tried calling him, but his phone number went straight to voicemail. She had an eerie feeling about all of it. Why had he left so abruptly with no goodbye? She remembered him talking so happily with her last night and there were no signs of him being unable to be with her anymore.

"You're my best friend." He had told her around 3 am, as they lay on her bed falling asleep. They had an amazing night and she wished it could have lasted forever. What had the morning brought

that the night hadn't? It felt uncharacteristic of the Peter she knew. It didn't make sense at all.

Betty couldn't believe she was back here again. She had broken up with James, and now Peter had just bolted? She felt ghosted and tossed away, a godforsaken mess.

Peter's ancient typewriter he had insisted on bringing over to her place was sitting on her desk. He had left it with a blank page ready to go.

Staring in disbelief at the typewriter and the old little poetry book sitting beside it, Betty took a seat at her desk. She felt like she had seen this film before. She opened up the book again and this time she saw that Peter had added another sentence to the first inscription he had written for her before.

Betty, I love you, it's ruining my life…
But I'll grow up and come back to find you someday!
Love, Peter

And just like that, it was clear Peter was gone, and he had left the book of tortured poems in the hands of a now-tortured Betty. It was now up to Peter to come back to her - and it felt like he was using Betty as a reason to grow up. She thought about how childish it was for him to leave her this way, like an unanswered question. Was it something she did?

Betty felt betrayed, deflated, and mystified.
So Betty did what she always did when she felt this way - she sat down and started writing.

She turned on her lamp, and began to type the title…

The Manuscript

How Did It End?

After August scolded Alison and ended it all, Alison sat on her bed crying in her dark room. It felt like August had taken a dagger and twisted it into her side. She was reeling with anger and mostly upset with herself for ever allowing herself to become attached to someone who was never hers.

Alison lit a match and held it tight between her thumb and finger. She stared as the small flame grew larger, inching closer to the skin on the tips of her fingers. There was something so calming about fire, she always felt peace while looking at it. She breathed through her tears, as she watched the flame grow and then die. She lit another one and imagined throwing it down on her room floor, tossing a bottle of whiskey down, watching the glass shattering and bursting into hot flames.

Dark memories of Alison's parents and how they were so quick to give up on her invaded Alison's mind. They had deemed her struggles too much for them and wanted only to pass her on to any doctor willing to fix her ailments. She had heard of the type of treatments they could do at the sanitarium and shuddered. She had escaped, but had she become better off? She now felt worse inside than ever before.

The candle on Alison's desk flickered. August knocked on her door, scaring her out of her deranged daydream. She opened it and felt his presence pierce through her chest. He stared at her, his face full of longing and sadness. He grabbed her and kissed her, holding her tight. Had he forgotten so quickly that he had just fired and dumped her?

August found himself in a haze of heartache and uncertainty. He wasn't sure why he had come back up to Alison's room - he didn't want to leave it like this. He couldn't take the thought of never seeing her again but knew there was no way he could keep her. It had to end.

Then it all happened so fast: the kiss, the push, the push back, and the lamp getting bumped off the desk and falling, rolling, the curtain lighting up with fire.

August panicked. The flames moved fast and there seemed to be no way to put them out before more spread further up the curtains. Heavy smoke began filling the tiny room very quickly. August decided he was powerless in putting it out and bolted - dragging Alison behind him, his hand gripped hard to hers as he yanked her towards the door.

"My book!" Screamed Alison as she yanked her hand out of August's tight grip. She ran back into the burning room.

Black smoke filled Alison's lungs as she let out a piercing scream, echoing throughout the hotel like music echoing across the waves of the ocean.

Everyone in the hotel awoke to the scream, warning them of the impending danger. August quickly ripped Lucy from her bed and yelled throughout the building for everyone to get out quickly.

The guests ran from the smoke and flames, as the building went up in mere minutes. It was a hot and windy night, and the strong gusts pushed the flames from the Albatross Hotel to the wooden buildings next door. Dark red and orange fire ravaged each building on Coney Island and acted as the catalyst for the next.

"Watch that one - she's here to destroy you." - August could hear the echoes of past voices within his head as he watched his beloved hotel burn behind him. He quickly ushered Lucy and his guests away from the flames.

Lucy's water had broken upon the panic and emergency of the fire, and her legs were now suddenly dripping with an uncomfortable fluid as she ran with August away from the smoke and searing heat.

August looked back up above the flames in the distance to see what could only be a large Albatross bird fly over the fire and towards the ocean - its giant wings flapping and fanning the flames below it. The bird appeared to be following them.

And that was the end of the Albatross Hotel - the so-called *"Lover House"*. Somehow rumors got out and spread quickly around Coney Island and New York that the devastating fire had been intentionally set in the Albatross Hotel by a young tortured artist named Alison. *"She was crazy." "She was a nutcase." "What a witch!" "A Mad Woman!"* The horrible things that people wrote to the paper about her character, as if they had the right to tear her to shreds over a baseless claim.

Early that morning, Lucy gave birth to a beautiful, premature baby girl. Her screams of labor and delivery terrified August, and the thought of losing Lucy now seemed incomprehensible. Yet August couldn't shake the feeling of Alison haunting him for what he did to her, casting shadows of bad omens about the entire hellish night, like a phantom hovering over them. He knew within his bones that he was responsible for all of it.

They named the baby Augustina. As August held his newborn daughter, he felt like the smallest man who ever lived. He had an immense sense of both grief and relief. The thought of Alison and how she might have died alone haunted him. He worried about his baby girl growing up in the same world in which he left Alison. He couldn't shake the feeling that he was the reason – that he had been the one to break her.

The night of the fire was the last time August ever saw Alison. But for the rest of his long life, he saw her face in strangers in crowded rooms, grocery store lineups, or a table at the same restaurant. Alison had marked him like a bloodstain.

When the smoke cleared and the hotel was a simmering mess, August went back to where Alison's room had once been. He felt sick to his stomach and needed to know if Alison was still alive.

August felt relieved to find no trace of her anywhere near where he left her in the fire, but sitting on what was left of the burnt wooden floor and ashes on the ground, he found a small homemade bound book sitting next to Alison's burnt and seared typewriter. The small book was titled simply, *The Manuscript*.

When August opened the book, out spilled poems and poems - both handwritten and typed. August held the book in his shaking hands, a souvenir of their entire torrid affair. A single charred piece of paper fell out and drifted to the ground.

When he read the words, the soft voice of Alison sang…

"I love you, it's ruining my life."

Lisa Rae Yamagishi lives in the Okanagan Valley in British Columbia, Canada. She spends all of her time with her 2 kids, 2 dogs, and her hilarious husband. She enjoys writing YA and Children's Fiction. She is a high school English and creative writing teacher, an avid snowboarder, and a lifelong Swiftie. Her goal is to make people feel connected and laugh with her books, and to become a full-time author someday.

The Manuscript is the sequel to *The Last Great American Dynasty.*
 Lisa is currently daydreaming ideas for a third and final book for *The Karma Collection* Series.

You can follow Lisa's tortured writing adventures on Instagram @LisaRaeYamz or TikTok @LisaRaeYamz or Twitter @LisaYamz

Eras Tour Vancouver Night 3!